When the Wind Blew

Petra Brown

Little Bear woke in the night. There was a sound. A big roaring sort of a sound. What could such a loud and scary sound be?

Little Bear growled and snuggled closer into Big Bear's warm belly.

"It's just the wind," said Big Bear. "It can't come in. We are safe and warm."

Soon the sound of the wind mingled with the sound of Big Bear's breathing and Little Bear drifted back to sleep.

"Good morning, little one!" Big Bear woke
Little Bear with a kiss on his nose.

Little Bear yawned and stretched. His tummy rumbled.
"I'm hungry," he said.

"Fat plums and honeycomb for breakfast?" asked Big Bear.

Little Bear licked his lips. "Mmmmmm!"

Big Bear pushed aside the
boulder at the mouth of their
den. Golden light rushed in.

"It's a very bright and sunny morning!"
said Big Bear, blinking at the light.

Little Bear let out a yelp and cried,
"All the trees are lying down!"

They looked in wonder at all the broken stumps and ragged roots. Yesterday the trees had stretched up to the sky, high above their heads. The leaves had cast shade all around. But this morning the sky was wide and bright and empty.

Big Bear gave a long, sad growl. "It must have happened in the night, while we were sleeping."

"Who did it?" asked Little Bear. "Who knocked all the trees over?"

"I guess it was the wind," said Big Bear. "There must have been a very big storm."

"I remember! I heard it roaring in the night!" said Little Bear. Suddenly his tummy gave a loud rumble. "Can we still have breakfast?" he asked.

Big Bear smiled and patted Little Bear on the head. "Well, we won't have to climb for honey or fruit today!"

After breakfast they went exploring. They climbed over, crawled under, and squeezed around the fallen trees, until they reached Mirror Lake where the water copied the sky.

"Did the wind hurt the water?" asked Little Bear.

"I guess it stirred it up into waves," said Big Bear, "but we can still drink it."

The water was cool and sweet.

"The birds must have had a terrible night!" said Big Bear.

"We're lucky," said Little Bear. "We sleep in a strong den, don't we?"

Big Bear nodded. "The birds will have to find new trees to roost in . . . and we will have to move, too."

"But why?" cried Little Bear.

"The fruit trees won't make fruit anymore, and the bees that make honey will fly away," said Big Bear. "They need trees to build their hives."

Little Bear felt upset and sad. Big Bear hugged him. "Don't worry, Little Bear, things will be fine . . . you wait and see."

Little Bear sat quietly thinking. *Things will be alright*, he thought . . .
as long as I have Big Bear.

"Come on, Little Bear. Let's ride the river!" Big Bear splashed into the
lake and lay down in the water, floating belly-up. Little Bear climbed
on top. Big Bear was like a big furry boat!

The river left Mirror Lake with a swoosh.

As he bobbed along on Big Bear's belly, Little Bear looked around him. Not one tree was left standing.

What if all the trees in the world had blown down?

Soon the river slowed and they swam ashore. Here was a pretty meadow. They lay among the sweet-smelling flowers and let the sun dry their fur.

"Why didn't the wind blow the flowers away?" asked Little Bear.

"They bend," said Big Bear, "and when the wind passes, they spring up again."

"I can bend," said Little Bear.

When they were dry they followed the river until they reached the edge of the cliffs where the waterfall made rainbows in the sun.

"Look!" cried Little Bear. "The trees in the valley are still standing!"

"I guess the cliff protected the trees from the wind," said Big Bear.

"If the wind blew now would it knock me down?"
Little Bear giggled.

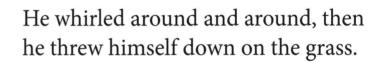

He whirled around and around, then
he threw himself down on the grass.

Big Bear bent down and swept him up in a hug.
"I would be like the cliff . . . I would protect you."

"I love you!" said Little Bear.

"And I love you!" said Big Bear.

They carefully made their way down the rocky cliffs. It was a long and scary climb!

There were narrow paths to tiptoe along.

There were wide gaps to jump.

There were bushes to hang from.

And after a while, there were trees to slide down.

At last they reached the forest floor, feeling very hot and tired.

The soft moss beneath their paws felt good. The cool shade all around from the tall trees felt very good. The air was filled with the wonderful smell of pine, sweet honey, and fruit.

And, among the scattered boulders at the foot of the cliffs, they found . . .

. . . a lovely, dry, dark cave!

"It's better than our old den!" cried Little Bear.

They gathered up grasses and flowers and made a big soft nest at the back of the cave.

By now the sky glowed orange through the trees. It was time for bed.

It had been a long and strange day and the two bears felt very sleepy. They cuddled up together, safe inside their new home.

"I don't miss our old den at all," said Little Bear as he snuggled up to Big Bear, "because when I'm with you, wherever we are, I feel I'm at home."

Big Bear's fur felt all warm and cozy around him, and Little Bear fell deeply and happily asleep.

For Mark
—*Petra*

Sleeping Bear Press™

2395 South Huron Parkway, Suite 200
Ann Arbor, MI 48104
www.sleepingbearpress.com

Printed and bound in the United States.

10 9 8 7 6 5 4 3 2 1

Library of Congress Cataloging-in-Publication Data

Names: Brown, Petra, author, illustrator.
Title: When the wind blew / written and illustrated by Petra Brown.
Description: Ann Arbor, MI : Sleeping Bear Press, [2017] |
Summary: "While Big Bear and Little Bear are sleeping, a wild storm rages.
They wake to find that the wind has knocked down the trees, they'll have to move.
Big Bear helps Little Bear understand that home is who you're with."
—Provided by the publisher.
Identifiers: LCCN 2016030983 | ISBN 9781585369690
Subjects: | CYAC: Bears—Fiction. | Home—Fiction. | Parent and child—Fiction.
Classification: LCC PZ7.B816683 Wh 2017 | DDC [E]—dc23
LC record available at https://lccn.loc.gov/2016030983